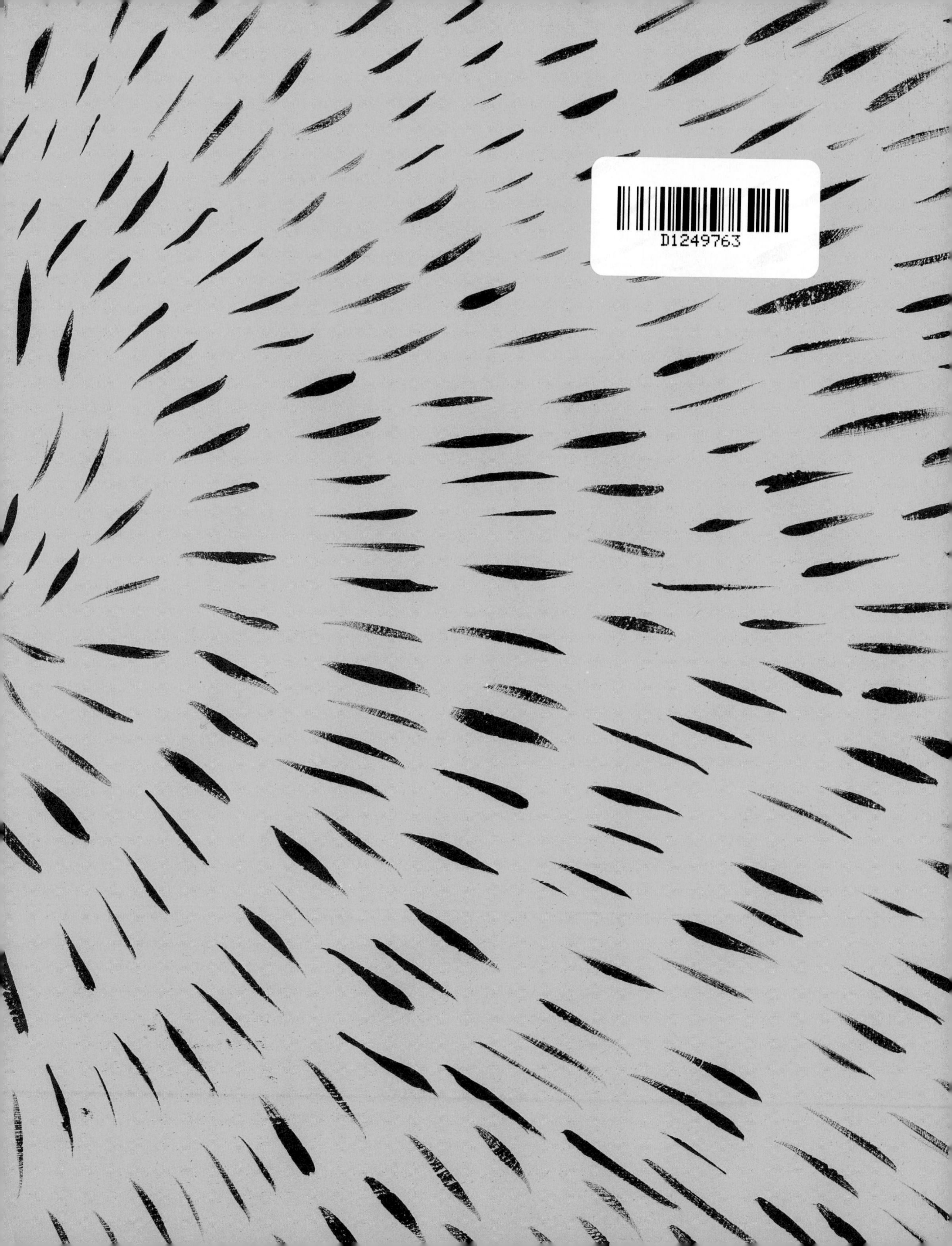
D1249763

For Lydia "Is it humid out? Look at my hair!" Ricci

The illustrations in this book were created with acrylic paint on BFK Rives printmaking paper with brushes that are made of imitation sable and inadvertently contain real strands of Lydia hair.

Cataloging-in-Publication Data has been applied for and may be obtained from the Library of Congress.

ISBN 978-1-4197-5190-5

Book design by Pamela Notarantonio

Printed and bound in China
10 9 8 7 6 5 4 3 2 1

ABRAMS The Art of Books
195 Broadway, New York, NY 10007
abramsbooks.com

INSIDE & OUT

A STORY ABOUT SMALL ACTS OF KINDNESS AND BIG HAIR

ZACHARIAH OHORA

Abrams Books for Young Readers
New York

Fuzzy Haskins was not
just a little fuzzy . . .

RIO

He was

SUPER FUZZY!

It took not one, but *two* hair dryers to dry him off after a bath.

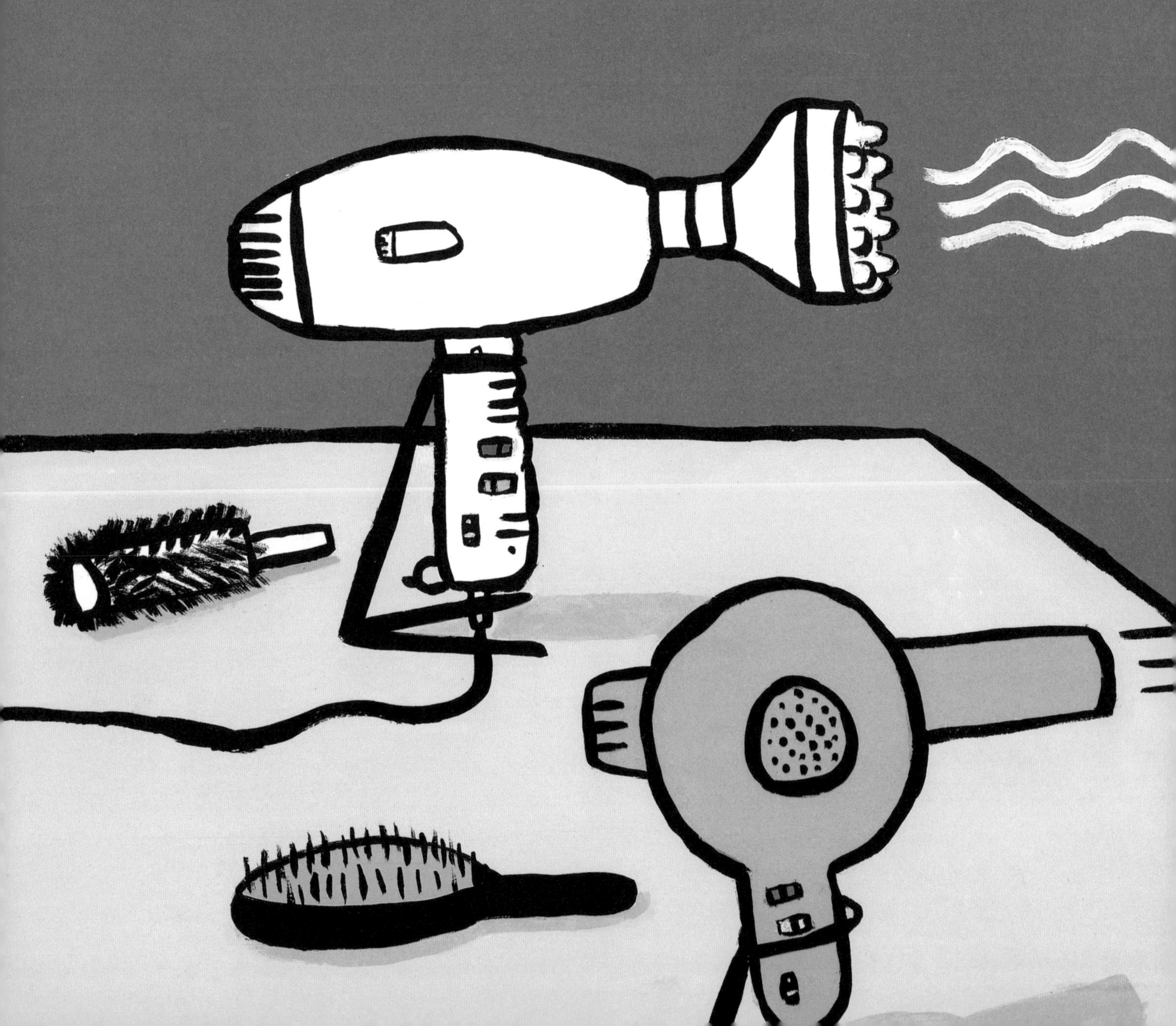

Fuzzy was on his way to bring cookies
to his best friend, Elise.

When Fuzzy floated by,
he smiled at everyone he saw . . .

and they smiled back.

This made him feel fuzzy, inside and out.

And he spread fuzziness wherever he went.

He helped in little ways for
things that were big . . .

Watch your step, Norm!
RIO

and he helped in big ways for things that were little.

Ooh!
Really!

Take these,
too. They
don't fit me
anymore.

Thanks,
Fuzzy!

He saved lost balloons.

And turned tears . . .

into cheers.

Uh-oh. Was that a drop of rain?
Fuzzy had been so busy helping out,
he hadn't noticed the darkening sky.

Rain is not a good thing when you're this fuzzy.

FWU

But the REAL problem is humidity!

It made it impossible for Fuzzy to see where he was going.

Smiles turned to frowns.

WHOOAH!

And Fuzzy’s world got turned upside down!

"Help!" yelped Fuzzy.

But he couldn't tell if anyone could hear him.

Now Fuzzy wasn't feeling fuzzy at all.
He was feeling stuck and alone.

But a little someone *did* hear him.

Who found the right someone . . .

. . . who told a big someone.

Together, they pulled with all their might.

Until . . .

Fuzzy was free!

His vision was a little fuzzy from being upside down so long. But after the stars faded, Fuzzy could see his good friends had rescued him.

But then Fuzzy looked at the cookies. “They’re smashed to bits!” he cried.

“Hmm . . .” murmured Elise. “I have an idea.”

No one had ever heard of cookie soup.

It turned out to be just cookie crumbs,
a splash of milk, some silly straws, and . . .

. . . sharing with a few good friends.

And that made **everyone** feel fuzzy.